For Christina Lucine, the girl who makes crystals shine bright

ORCHARD BOOKS
Carmelite House
50 Victoria Embankment
London EC4Y 0DZ

First published in 2016 in the United States
by Little, Brown and Company

This edition published by Orchard Books in 2017

HASBRO and its logo, MY LITTLE PONY and all related characters are
trademarks of Hasbro and are used with permission.

© 2017 Hasbro. All rights reserved.

A CIP catalogue record for this book is available
from the British Library.

ISBN 978 1 40834 466 8

1 3 5 7 9 10 8 6 4 2

Printed in Great Britain

Orchard Books
An imprint of Hachette Children's Group
Part of The Watts Publishing Group Limited
An Hachette UK Company
www.hachette.co.uk

Princess Cadance

✱ ✱ and ✱ ✱

The Glitter Heart Garden

Written by G. M. Berrow

ORCHARD

Contents

CHAPTER 1

Heartsong

Princess Cadance sighed. This Heartsong hadn't gone at all as she had hoped. Usually, the annual Hearts and Hooves Day Heartsong had so many ponies in attendance that not everypony could fit in the main square! Ponies of all ages would spill out on to the shimmering side streets. They would bring apple crates to stand on, craning their necks for a glimpse of the Crystal Heart and the popular young royals conducting the songs. This year, however, a horrible case of the pony sniffles had swept across the kingdom. Most of the residents were at home, snuggled in their beds.

Princess Cadance knew that it was a major problem, for the Heartsong was actually a very important event. If the Crystal Heart didn't receive regular bursts of light and love from the ponies of the land, it might break again and the entire kingdom would be in grave danger.

The Frozen North was always looming. After the recent events when the Crystal Heart had actually broken apart, Princess Cadance wasn't taking any chances with its health. The incident had already made this winter much more frigid and blustery than the Empire was accustomed to, and the grounds had seen better days.

It was imperative that the Crystal Heart be pumped full of love at all times. Otherwise, the entire Crystal Empire could be lost to the icy avalanches.

Cadance took a few steps toward the sparse crowd of Crystal Empire citizens. She shot a private, nervous look at her husband, Prince Shining Armour. The striking stallion replied with his signature encouraging nod. His blue mane fell over his eyes. *You can do it*, he assured her without even speaking. Princess Cadance nodded back. She felt braver now. Shining Armour always had that effect on her.

"Dearest Crystal ponies!" Cadance addressed the small crowd. "Every Hearts and Hooves Day,

we join together so our love will warm us through the few remaining days of our frosty winter and carry us into our beautiful spring." Cadance pointed daintily at the Crystal Heart. Her candy-coloured mane gently swayed in the winter wind.

"I thank you for sharing your voices and hearts with your fellow ponies on this special day!" The princess mustered a sunny smile. "Your kindness and love for one another rings true through each note and melody. I deliver my warm wishes to you and all your loved ones at home with the pony sniffles."

"And now, one last song!" called Shining Armour as he trotted forward.

The royal baby, Princess Flurry Heart, rode on her father's back. She bounced along with her oversized wings outstretched, and giggled at each bumpy hoofstep. The crowd cooed. Shining Armour laughed as he addressed the citizens. "It's Flurry Heart's favourite!" Cadance signalled to the Crystal Sym-pony Orchestra, and a rich tune began to fill the air around them. The distinct opening notes of the Crystal flugelhorn trumpeted. Flurry squealed happily.

When the Crystal Snow gets icy
and chilly
Join voices with every colt
and every filly!
There's only one solution,
And we've made a resolution.

We'll lift our spirits to the sky.
Our hearts grow full and our
hooves rise up high.
Hooves cold, hearts warm;
cold hooves, warm hearts!
Hearts and Hooves Day,
we all take part!

Despite the small group, the voices grew strong as the song hit the crescendo. On the highest note, multiple bright bursts of light shot straight toward the Crystal Heart! A warm, happy feeling washed over everypony's glittering, crystalline face. As Princess Cadance scanned the contented kingdom, she knew that everything was going to be all right. Maybe it didn't matter after all that most of the ponies were at home, slurping get-well soup. The love in the Crystal Empire was safe for another season. As the song came to an end,

Cadance looked out at the shimmering buildings built with sturdy crystal and reminded herself that their home was stronger than it appeared.

"This Hearts and Hooves Day was just as awesome as the rest." Shining Armour lifted Flurry Heart from his back and placed her gently in the foal stroller. "See, Mi Amore?"

"You know I don't like to be called that name." Cadance frowned and nudged the stallion. She leaned down and tucked a soft blanket around Flurry Heart. The baby smiled, her big eyes blinking.

"I know – that's why I do it," he replied with a satisfied laugh. "But honestly, Cadance, don't you agree that maybe you were worrying a little too much about the Heartsong? It all turned out perfectly."

"I suppose you're right," Cadance admitted. "Still, I just hope everypony gets better soon."

"So do I," Shining Armour agreed, motioning toward the castle with his horn. "Now, let's go home and have a nice, quiet evening *inside*, where it's toasty warm. My flanks are freezing out here!" Shining Armour could be a baby colt when it came to chilly weather.

Winter was his least favourite season, so naturally he liked to remind everypony of that all the time – another reason why Cadance couldn't wait until the bright sunshine of spring melted the snow and ice away. She shook her head, mildly amused at her husband shivering dramatically in an attempt to get sympathy.

"Let's go and warm you up," Cadance teased as she took one last glance at the Crystal Heart. Flurry Heart pointed her tiny hoof at it and gurgled. "What is it, sweetie?" Cadance asked.

A group of five ponies who had been gathering near the gem waited patiently nearby. They hung back, pretending to inspect the facets up close, but the princess could read body language well enough to know that they were waiting to say hello to her. A teenaged Unicorn filly with a pink mane and a grumpy expression caught Cadance's eye. The mint-green pony was shuffling her hooves around and looking off into the distance. There was something familiar about her, but Cadance couldn't quite put her hoof on it.

"Actually, you take Flurry Heart and go ahead. Get the fire started," Cadance instructed her husband as she kept her eyes on the curious group. "I'll be along shortly to make you two some hot chocolate. I just need to take care of something first."

"Hot chocolate with marshmallows?" Shining Armour's face lit up with a giant smile, and he galloped off toward the castle. "My wife is the best!"

Princess Cadance laughed as she trotted back over to the Crystal Heart.

She had taken only a few steps before the group of ponies launched themselves right in front of her.

"Your Majesty!" exclaimed the leader of the group, a tall lavender mare with a cutie mark of a bunch of Crystal berries. She had her golden mane in the traditional updo of the region, with sparkling purple bands across her head. Once the mare opened her mouth, the words came rushing out.

"It is so lovely to see you, and may I say what a beautiful Heartsong that was? I haven't seen such a small turnout since I was a filly during the year that almost everypony travelled to the big Hearts and Hooves event in Canterlot. My mother wouldn't let me go. I don't think I even had my cutie mark yet! Wow, time flies, doesn't it? It feels as if it's been a thousand years – well, technically it has been, I suppose. Ha! Get it? Because of King Sombra? Oh, listen to me rambling again!" The mare laughed. A young green filly rolled her eyes and followed it with a heavy sigh. The purple mare didn't notice, or chose to ignore it. "Anyhow, I don't know if you remember me, but I'm—"

"Lilac Quartz?" Cadance finished for her. As soon as the mare had begun talking, Cadance had recognised her, which was a relief because the princess prided herself on trying to recall the names of everypony she met. "Of course I remember you. You run the Crystal Crown Café!" Memories of the delicious meals at the charming spot suddenly made her very hungry. "Do you still make that delectable carrot-ginger soup?

It was my absolute favourite thing to eat when I first arrived in the Crystal Empire."

Lilac Quartz blushed. The chatty mare was speechless!

"Yes, they do," chimed in one of her friends, Rose Water, with a massive grin. "You and the prince should *definitely* stop by sometime soon." Something about the delivery of her comment made Cadance think that the mare cared more about Shining Armour's presence than hers.

"*I* shall," Princess Cadance replied warmly with a little bow of her head. "And I can't wait to see that little filly of yours again, Lilac. She was so adorable, always covered in flour from baking Crystal berry tarts. How is she?"

"Your Majesty, you can ask my Olivine Jewel herself." Lilac Quartz smiled as she pointed her hoof at the moody young filly. "She's right there."

"My stars!" Cadance breathed in awe. "She's all grown up." Olivine Jewel was now staring at the Crystal Heart and frowning. She paced impatiently, clopping her hooves on the ground.

"Oh dearie," Lilac Quartz tutted, leaning in closer to Cadance to whisper. "Between you and me, Princess, she's not the same little filly she used to be. All doom and gloom with her these days, I'm afraid. Everything is either boring or embarrassing. Teenagers, you know?" Lilac's friends all shook their heads in support.

"And still no cutie mark …" commented Sweet Leaf.

Rose Water sighed. "And Olivine doesn't even like coming into the Crystal Crown Café any more."

"I'm sure it's just a phase ..." Cadance made a sympathetic face. She wasn't sure what to say to make the exhausted mother feel any better. It was true that Cadance herself used to be an expert on foal-sitting, but becoming a mother to Flurry Heart had been an entirely

 different endeavour. It was exhausting and confusing, but also the most wonderful experience that the princess could recall in her whole life. Cadance's heartstrings were wrapped tightly around her little foal. No doubt Lilac Quartz felt the same about her Olivine.

"Well, isn't *that* interesting!" Olivine Jewel shouted not two seconds later.

She perked up, eyes bright, but remained focused on the Crystal Heart. "Mama, hurry over!"

"What is it, Olive?" Lilac Quartz brightened and trotted over, her three friends in tow. The mares crowded Cadance's view, but several shrieks suddenly escaped from the group. When the mares parted and Cadance saw what they were looking at, she almost shrieked as well.

The soft blue light of the special gemstone was beating very slowly, almost coming to a complete stop. The Crystal Heart was dying!

CHAPTER 2

Matters of the Crystal Heart

Princess Cadance burst into her living quarters, adrenaline coursing through her body as she scanned the cavernous space for her husband and foal. Cadance couldn't believe that her worst fears about today had come true after all. She was lucky that she'd stayed behind to talk with the group of mares and fillies. Otherwise she wouldn't have seen the dying Crystal Heart in time. Cadance had managed to boost the energy of the Heart with her powerful Alicorn magic, but it wouldn't last for ever. She needed another plan.

Cadance cantered through the halls of the castle even faster.

The Crystal Heart was in terrible danger, and if she didn't fix it soon, the Crystal Empire would be, too. All she'd wanted was to see the ponies of her land filled with light and love and to watch the kingdom blossom into a beautiful spring – bees buzzing, pretty flowers blooming and ponies prancing around and playing together. If the Heart stopped glowing and broke apart once more, there would never be spring again. The entire expanse and everypony in it would be covered with much worse than the normal winter – it would be an avalanche of snow from the Frozen North!

"Shining Armour!" the princess cried out as she galloped toward the couple's sitting room, where the fireplace was. "We have a problem! The Crystal Hea— *Whoaaaaa!*" As if in slow motion, Cadance lost her hoofing. As she fell to the ground, she managed to glimpse the culprit responsible for her ungraceful tumble. It was one of her gowns from a past gala. She'd tried it on earlier to see if she wanted to send it to Rarity for alterations and had carelessly tossed it on to the floor.

The moment Cadance hit the floor, she expected to hear a loud *thud*. But the impact made no sound at all because the princess had landed on a patch of grass. She looked up to see that she was now in a soft green garden with the sun shining on her pink face. The fresh air held the heavy, pleasant scent of flower blossoms. In the distance, intricate topiaries lined the horizon. Hundreds of ponies were laughing and singing. Where was she? A searing flash of blue momentarily blinded her, and she was back in the sitting room with her hoof tangled up in a gown.

"Cadance! What are you doing on the floor?" Shining Armour bolted over to help his wife, ditching the pile of logs he'd assembled. "Are you hurt?" Shining Armour reached out his hoof.

"No, no. I'm all right … but

I *am* confused," Cadance mused, trying to work out what exactly she had just seen. Had it been a dream? A premonition? Or had it just been her most sincere wish that had appeared to tease her? A beautiful spring day in the Crystal Empire garden…

"Confused?" Shining Armour asked with a sly smirk, picking up the dress from the floor and holding it up as evidence. "About why you are the most beautiful, prim-and-proper princess, but also secretly also the *messiest* mare in all of the Crystal Empire?" He chuckled lovingly. He had not known that side of Cadance until they were married. Shining Armour's belongings were displayed neatly on his shelves, whereas Cadance's things were everywhere! The princess had many admirable qualities, but tidiness was not one of them.

When Cadance didn't giggle at his jab as she usually did, Shining Armour knew something was off. "What is it, Cady? You look kind of strange. *Kind of* like you just had—"

"One of my visions," Cadance confirmed, her almond-shaped eyes widening as she met his. She nodded in disbelief. "I can't figure it out. It's been years since I've had any that strong, and now *two* in one day!"

Ever since she was a little Pegasus filly, Cadance had received hazy visions of the future. They were random and uncontrollable, but they were almost always fulfilled. After many years of observing the unique magical ability as she watched Cadance grow, Princess Celestia believed the talent had come to Cadance through Prismia, the evil enchantress Cadance had defeated as a young pony. Not many ponies knew of this gift. Of course, Shining Armour was one of the few who did. Princess Cadance could keep nothing from her best friend.

"Whoa, two visions?" Shining Armour cocked his head.

"This morning, before the Heartsong, I saw another. It was why I was so worried about everypony being too sick to join in," she admitted. She let out a heavy sigh and trotted over to her favorite cushy chair, hoping to find some respite. "I saw the Crystal Heart. The light went completely out of it, just like it had when Sombra ruled." She shuddered thinking about the fight against the evil tyrant stallion who once enslaved the

Crystal ponies under his wretched rule.

"Aw, Cadance. I *know* it's taken a long time for the Crystal ponies to recover from that nasty dude, but we're safe now." He patted her hoof. Shining Armour was such an optimist sometimes. "We should do our best to forget about him."

"I love your positivity, Shiny dearest," Cadance replied kindly. "But I'm afraid I disagree. Even if King Sombra never returns, we still must look to the Crystal Heart to protect us." Cadance stood up, determined. "And I'm going to make sure it happens. It's my duty as reigning princess of  this land – *our* duty – to be absolutely sure everypony is safe not only today, but always!"

"Well, I can't argue with my clever wife on *that*," Shining Armour admitted. "But how are we going to do it?"

"By fulfilling my other vision, of course." Cadance smiled, thinking of the old garden on the outskirts of the castle grounds. She'd never actually visited it, but she had heard ponies speak about the area from time to time.

"The Crystal Empire is clearly destined to have an amazing celebration in the garden, and I'm going to make it happen. The ponies are going to be filled with so much love and light that we'll never have to worry again!" Cadance rose and did a little victory twirl. Her violet, rose and gold mane billowed out like a flouncy skirt.

"Cool with me." Shining Armour shrugged with a smile. "But can we at least have that hot chocolate first?"

Chapter 3

Castle Grounded

The next morning felt much warmer than the previous one. Princess Cadance took it as a good indication that winter would be over soon – perfect timing to execute her brilliant idea. As she trotted across the castle grounds to go and inspect the venue with Shining Armour, Cadance began to brainstorm all the ways to make this second Heartsong a success. Along with fragrant flowers and sunshine, there would have to be topiaries, of course – she'd seen that much in her vision. The rest of the details were open to improvisation. They could hold a parade, with floats decorated entirely with fresh flowers! And perhaps she'd commission the bakers to make a violet cream cake …

"Hurry up, Shining Armour," Cadance urged. "We have so much to do!"

The couple wasn't even halfway to the garden before they were interrupted. A beefy stallion from the Royal Guard galloped over, looking precise and perfect as ever. He was out of breath. "Your Majesties," he said with a bow, "I do beg your pardon … but I have … an important scroll … from Princess Celestia."

"It's no problem at all." Cadance returned his bow. "Thank you for your promptness in delivering it. Where is the scroll?"

"Apologies, Princess," the guard said, blushing, "but the scroll is meant for Commander Shining Armour's eyes only. Royal Guard business. Strict instructions."

The prince, who was still a bit bleary-eyed, straightened as if he were under inspection by an invisible chief commander. "Really?" He used the magic from his Unicorn horn to unfurl it and quickly scanned the contents. Whatever it was, his expression was quite serious.

"Bad news?" Cadance pried, leaning in her pink muzzle to sneak a peek.

But Shining Armour rolled it back up quickly before she was able to make out anything on the page.

Shining Armour smoothed down his messy blue mane. "It's just pretty much that I've been told to hold our new Royal Guard recruitment trials early. Celestia wants me to start right away."

"What a strange request …" Cadance tilted her head, causing her golden crown to glint in the morning sunlight. "Did she say why?" The princesses didn't normally keep things from one another. Not unless there was a good reason.

"No, she just explained that it was 'important' to take precautions." Shining Armour pulled Cadance into a hug. "But I've got it all taken care of, so *don't worry*." He leaned in and touched his Unicorn horn to Cadance's, nuzzling her face.

He lowered his voice to a whisper. "Please get somepony to help you with all this. I know how you like to do everything yourself, but I don't want you to wear yourself out …"

"You worry far too much," Princess Cadance said with a smile and a wink. "I'm perfectly capable. Besides, it'll be really simple! Just a few decorations and we'll be ready for spring."

"OK …" Shining Armour lifted a brow. "But just leave the training fields alone?"

"Nope, I'm decorating those, too!" she teased as she waved at Shining Armour and his guard. Then Cadance set off to finish the task at hoof, feeling more excited with each trot. This was going to be so much fun, and the perfect way to power the Crystal Heart.

A crumbling signpost in the near distance guided the way. It read: EMPIRE GARDEN, BY MASTER GARDENER "A.S." Cadance followed the arrow and came upon a set of partially shattered crystal gates. As she gingerly pushed them open and pranced inside, the pink princess gasped at her surroundings, utterly speechless because of what she saw. It certainly was a sight to behold, but not the nice one she'd expected. Instead of a well-manicured place to frolic and play, the garden was a complete mess!

CHAPTER 4

A Growing Idea

How in Equestria did this happen? Cadance
thought as she began to explore the
withered area. Everywhere the princess
looked, there were rows upon rows of
overgrown hedges, dead flowers and piles
of dirt. Instead of the golden pots meant to
contain the topiaries shaped like animals,

all Cadance found were some large ceramic vessels with broken, peeling tree stems.

As she wandered, Cadance wondered if she had read it all wrong. Perhaps her vision was supposed to be taking place in a different area of the grounds. Or maybe it was not her destiny at all. It was quite possible that the sad, old garden was just what it appeared to be – hopeless and broken. But on the other hoof, with some extra love it *could* be blossoming in no time. Cadance smiled, coming to a realisation. Love was always the answer.

The princess closed her violet eyes and

inhaled. The air was still fresh and the warm sun was still shining on her face. That was plenty to get started!

A few hours into her work on cleaning up the garden, a couple of things were becoming clear to the princess: she didn't know very much about landscaping or gardening, and this project was going to be a much bigger task than she'd anticipated. Even with the aid of her strong magic to help her lift, move and dig things, she was still just one pony. Cadance was going to need some helping hooves. *Fast.*

A murmur of voices nearby disrupted Cadance's quiet moment. Across the massive expanse of grass, a large group of young teenage fillies and colts followed a castle tour guide. An older mare with a red mane led the way. She was chatting and calling out to the group. The young ponies hardly paid attention because they were too busy whispering with their friends or daydreaming.

It reminded Cadance of her days living back in Canterlot with Princess Celestia and Princess Luna. Sometimes Cadance helped out by giving tours around the castle to school groups. The young ponies would always drag their hooves in boredom through the whole thing until the very end of the day – when they got to help cook a meal for their class in the castle kitchens. The ponies would suddenly become engaged and playful when they had a way to contribute.

Princess Cadance left the garden and headed

straight for the tour group with a seed of an idea growing in her head. She needed extra hooves, and the group needed something to occupy themselves with.

"Welcome to the castle!" Princess Cadance called out. Everypony turned to look at her, quite surprised to find the princess covered in soil and wandering around by herself. "Pardon my appearance," Cadance laughed, trotting up closer to them, "but I've just been working on a little project down at the garden, and I heard voices."

"Your Majesty!" the tour guide mare gasped, and bowed. "I was just taking this school group around to the back entrance. If I'd known you were here, we could have taken a different route—"

"Don't be silly, Petal Shine," replied Cadance, picking a leaf out of her mane. "I'm actually extremely glad to see all of you!" She scanned the faces of the young ponies. They all looked a little starstruck except for … Olivine Jewel. The green filly stood at the back of the group on her own, wearing her permanent grumpy expression. Cadance smiled at her. "Hello, Olivine!"

At this, Olivine's entire class and teacher spun around to look at the young filly, shocked. A blush appeared on her cheeks as the ponies began to whisper to one another. How did the princess know Olivine?

"It is so lovely to meet you, Your Majesty. I'm Ruby Jubilee!" The teacher stepped up to Princess Cadance and gave a rather wobbly curtsey. "And this is my class.

We're exploring careers at the castle today! Do you have any tips for our little ponies?"

"Just follow your hearts," offered Cadance warmly. "It always leads to the right decision, if you listen."

"Splendid advice. Thank you, Princess!" Ruby Jubilee cooed. "Hear that, class? Princess Cadance—"

"But what about following your cutie mark?" a stocky blue colt with a shaggy mane called out. "Isn't that what we're supposed to do?" His cutie mark was a picture of a mop.

Olivine began to shuffle her hooves. She kicked a clump of dirt.

"Yeah! That is what we're supposed to do," called out a yellow filly with a muffin cutie mark. A few other ponies nodded in agreement. Ruby Jubilee shot them all a stern teacher look. "Mop Top, Citrine—

Let's not bother the princess with too
many questions."

"Oh, I don't mind!" Cadance knew
to choose her words carefully. "Your cutie
marks are definitely
important, but some very
special fillies in Ponyville
recently helped remind
me that a cutie mark is
just one part of you.

Everypony can be wonderful at all sorts of
things. You just have to try!" Cadance
produced a scroll from her saddlebag and
unfurled it. It was a rough map of the
garden. "For example, how would you all
like to try something new with me? I'm
planning a big, beautiful garden
celebration in honour of spring, and I
would love for you all to come and
join me."

The teacher's jaw dropped. "You want *my* Crystal Preparatory students to help you with your special project?" Ruby Jubilee squealed with delight. "Wow! Why, of course they would love to! It would be such an honour!" Another wave of whispers broke out among the students, but this time they sounded like excited ones.

"That's wonderful news!" Cadance sighed in relief. "Now all we need is to tell the rest of the kingdom."

"And do *all* the work," muttered Olivine. "*Or* you could just hire a professional gardener pony."

But nopony listened to her, as usual.

CHAPTER 5

Helping Hooves

By the time Princess Cadance made it
down to the garden the next morning,
the young ponies had been up for hours
and the work was in full swing. Cadance's
heart felt full as she watched the progress
that had been made by the hooves of
Crystal Empire citizens. They had already
begun repainting the pots a shimmering
gold colour and started digging up weeds,

and were digging the soil to make a nice bed for brand-new plants.

The teacher, Ruby Jubilee, marched around with the scroll in her hoof trying to match Cadance's plans to the tasks everypony was assigned. Mop Top and Citrine were currently working together to weave rainbow ribbons and white lights into the roof of the old gazebo. Below the pair, a pink Unicorn named Gemma and a golden Earth pony called Sweet Éclair were coating the gazebo with white paint. The two ponies whistled happily as they wielded their brushes, laughing every so often when one of them accidentally splashed paint on to the other.

Even though the work was tough, the ponies seemed happy to be doing something important. Princess Cadance grabbed a shovel and started helping out.

She felt lucky to have stumbled upon such a lovely group of ponies. She was having so much fun, too!

When some castle attendants came down to fetch the princess for some important state business, Cadance didn't want to go. She felt terrible about leaving her new helpers, but Ruby Jubilee had insisted that her class would be just fine carrying on without her.

Duty calls, Cadance thought, vowing to come back as soon as possible.

Over by a row of flower beds, Olivine Jewel frowned and shook her head as she watched the royal trot back toward the castle. "She's *leaving*? Who does she think she is?" she complained.

"Duh, Olive, a *princess*," said an orange mare named Fire Opal as she plopped another giant Funflower into the soil. Her rainbow-striped mane had pieces of dirt and leaves sticking out of it. "She has tons of other work to do instead of gardening. Besides, I bet it's all boring meetings and stuff. She probably wants to stay here with us because it's so awesome!"

"It's very enjoyable," agreed Star Seed. The purple Unicorn with a wavy blue mane closed her eyes, smiling. "I'm feeling so in tune with nature … It's making me really relaxed." Star Seed stifled a big yawn.

"No, Star," Olivine snapped back. "You're tired because we're all being *forced* to do community service for the castle! It's so unfair."

"Olive, why do you always have to be

such a grump? We're *not* being forced. We *want* to help Princess Cadance with the garden," replied Fire Opal, a hint  of annoyance in her voice.

"The celebration is going to be the best ever. Did you hear we are going to have a parade where all the floats are covered completely with flowers?"

"Really?" Star Seed perked up. "That's so cool." She closed her eyes again and sat down on the grass.

"Plus," Fire Opal continued, "Princess Cadance said we could use 'artistic licence' and plant whatever flowers we want. I think it's really neat of her to let us design stuff for the castle. It's good experience."

"I have an idea. Let's try to make our sections of the garden really unique …"

Star Seed said dreamily as she looked up at the clouds. "Like, pretty and weird at the same time, you know?"

"I love that!" Fire Opal chirped. "Then the ponies who want something a little different can come to our spot."

"Whatever. I hate this garden." Olivine kicked a shovel with her hoof. "It's no use trying to fix it anyway. It's never going to be like it was before King Sombra."

"Yeah, right." Fire Opal rolled her eyes. "Like *you* actually remember what it was like before King Sombra."

"Yes, I do!" Olivine stood up, growing annoyed. Her pink mane frizzed out around her face, making her look a little frantic. "And if we actually tried to re-create it … the garden would look way better than this mess. I … I … can show you how it used to look to prove it!"

"How?" Fire Opal and Star Seed exchanged an unconvinced look. It was well known that Olivine was always throwing fits over the tiniest things and making up stories for attention. It was probably because she didn't have her cutie mark yet, but it's not as if anypony ever teased her about that. The real reason why nopony liked to hang out with Olivine was because she was so moody.

"Just come with me and I'll show you," Olivine said, sounding sincere and calm for once. "Please?"

CHAPTER 6

The Greenhouse

The crumbling cottage was all the way on the outskirts of the city, tucked away near a shimmering Crystal lake. It was chillier than the centre of the Empire, so there was still a light frost covering every surface. Olivine hadn't told Fire Opal and Star Seed who they were going to visit.

They just knew that the pony in question was very mysterious. The three ponies crouched in the Crystal berry bushes near the front door.

"So who lives here?" Fire Opal whispered. "Can you tell us now?" Her eyes were alight with intrigue. "A zebra who can concoct potions? A bat-pony? Daring Do?"

"My grandpa," Olivine said reverently, a sparkle in her eye. She crouched low as she trotted to the front door, signalling for the others to follow her. "Come on!"

"Your *what*?" Fire Opal stood up, no longer caring about keeping quiet. She turned to Star Seed. "Is she joking right now? Did she bring us all this way to visit her *grandpa*?"

Star Seed shrugged and popped a berry into her mouth. Nothing fazed her.

They'd come this far. The two ponies had no choice but to follow Olive through the door.

"*Shhh!*" Olive hissed when it slammed closed behind Star Seed. "We can't wake him." She gestured to an old stallion, snoozing peacefully in a big velvet chair. His glasses were one snore away from falling off his muzzle, and his white mane frizzed out in every direction, just like Olivine's.

"I just need to find one thing from here," whispered Olive, tip-hoofing through the room. "Don't touch anything!"

The old house was packed with shelves upon shelves of well-loved, dusty books and hundreds of potted plants of every variety. The warm temperature and the sunlight streaming in through the skylight made it feel just like a cosy greenhouse. Star Seed, who seemed to like it, started looking through one of the bookshelves.

As the Unicorn scanned the titles, she began to notice a theme. Almost all the books were about plants, seeds, or spells! She ran her hoof gently along the spines and picked one that was displayed prominently, entitled *Indigenous Magical Plants of the North and South, Volume 5: Flowers.* She was reading about a strange magical flower called a Lazilily, which supposedly filled ponies with lethargy, when somepony called out her name. Star Seed put the book down on the table and quickly trotted to join the others outside. Olivine and Fire Opal were staring at a small wooden box full of tiny pouches.

Fire Opal crinkled her nose. "What are they?"

"Supposedly, they're magical seeds,"
Olivine explained with a grin. She picked
up a blue pouch and poured a few
shimmering specks out on to her hoof.
"My grandpa, Alabaster, has been
collecting them for ever. He always said
that if planted, they would grow into the
prettiest and *weirdest* flowers ever."

"I like the sound of that," Star Seed said,
nodding in approval. "But *how* weird?"

"And what makes them magical?" Fire
Opal raised a suspicious eyebrow. For the
first time ever, there was a flicker of real
excitement in Olivine's eyes.

"I don't know. But we're going to plant
them in the castle garden and find out!"

CHAPTER 7

Float On

The air outside was warm enough for the doors leading to the balcony in Cadance and Shining Armour's castle bedroom to be kept open. A gentle breeze floated through the space as the princess got ready for dinner. Cadance hummed a tune to herself while brushing her long, soft mane into its pretty curls. She placed her pretty golden crown on top of her head.

It had felt like ages since she and her husband had been able to carve out the time to sit down together for a real meal. And now that baby Flurry Heart was old enough to stay with the castle foal-sitter, the young royals could finally have a moment for each other.

"May I escort the lovely mare to the dining room?" Shining Armour appeared at the doorway wearing a white waistcoat, with a cheesy grin on his face. He nodded in a formal bow so low that his blue mane nearly touched the floor.

"You may." Cadance stifled a giggle and bowed back. "But please make it quick, because this lovely mare is absolutely starving!"

Shining Armour laughed and held his hoof out to his wife. Cadance was in good spirits, so he was happy.

When they got to the main castle dining room, two places at the end of the banquet table were already set. A butler pony was waiting with a bottle of fresh apple juice. He motioned to the setup with a flourish and began to pour them each a glass.

"I feel relieved to see you smiling," admitted Shining Armour once they'd sat down at the massive table. "Sorry I've been so busy with the Royal Guard recruitment trials lately. It's just really important that we have a strong team, especially this year."

"I understand," Cadance assured him. She still wondered about the contents of the letter from Princess Celestia, though.

Needing more security for the Crystal Empire could mean that there was a potential threat. "But is everything OK?"

"Of course! How is the garden coming along?" Shining Armour queried, his mouth full of salad. "Are your student helpers having fun out there? Sure seems like it! I just saw three little ponies still digging around on my way here. Isn't it getting a bit late?"

"I know. Those little ponies have been so dedicated. Every time I go to the garden, they are planting more gorgeous, exotic flowers. I'm not sure how they are getting them to grow so fast, but it's amazing." Cadance scrunched up her nose. "I wanted to watch and learn their green-hoof secrets, but for some reason they don't seem to want any extra help from me."

"They probably know you've got your hooves full as it is, sweetie."

"Well, they *are* right about that," Cadance admitted as she took a sip of apple juice. "There's still so much else to do to prepare. Besides the new garden, there's the maypole, the parade, the Heartsong music …"

Shining Armour's eyes grew wide. "Whoa there, filly! A parade, too?"

"A parade will only help spread the love throughout the entire Crystal Empire," the princess said. "Ponies have already been visiting the garden to collect flowers to use on their entries for the floral float competition." Cadance's pretty almond-shaped eyes sparkled with delight. "You should see some of the designs!

They are so beautiful and bright. Just what everypony needs to lift their spirits."

"That's awesome, Cady," commended Shining Armour. His face showed concern. "But do you think it will boost the Crystal Heart like you were hoping?"

Princess Cadance beamed. She had saved the best news for last.

"It already has."

"This isn't really what I pictured when you said the Crystal Heart got a boost …" Shining Armour craned his neck and gawked at the elaborate float. The structure looked like a giant version of the Crystal Heart, except this one was half covered with flowers. A group of ponies was busy attaching even more blooms.

"I know." Princess Cadance motioned with her pink hoof. "But don't the ponies look happy?"

Shining Armour nodded. He couldn't deny what he saw. "Totally!"

"Well, that's what's helping the Heart." Cadance trotted away and Shining Armour followed. She cantered past several other floats shaped like everything from giant flowers to Crystal berry cupcakes. Everything was covered in fragrant, fresh flowers. They smelled heavenly.

"Come and look!"

Shining Armour and Princess Cadance approached the real Crystal Heart. It was suspended below the castle, as usual. But its strength was visibly steadier, glowing bright blue and flickering only every couple of minutes.

"It's still not enough, but I haven't had to use my magic to boost it again," Cadance explained. "The Garden Hearts Celebration is going to fix everything for good. I just *know* it."

"Your Majesty!" cried an aqua-coloured mare, galloping up to the couple. Her face showed distress. "I'm so glad you're here. We have an emergency – it's Petal Shine!"

"What is it, Emerald Gem?" Cadance snapped into alert mode. "Is she hurt?"

"Not exactly, but I think you should come and look for yourself …"

They raced over. The purple pony was lying on the ground, holding her stomach.

At first, Petal Shine appeared to be shivering. But upon closer inspection, it became clear that the pony was just in a fit of uncontrollable giggles. "Can't … stop … hee hee! Ha ha!" Petal Shine squirmed and wiggled. "Oh my! Ha ha ha ha!"

"What's so funny, Petal Shine?" Cadance was stumped. She hadn't heard a joke that hilarious in ages. Watching Petal Shine laugh so hard made her giggle herself. "Please share it with us!"

"No, Princess." Emerald Gem frowned, shaking her head. "You misunderstand … Petal Shine has been like this for *hours*, and we can't figure out why."

Shining Armour tried to help Petal Shine up from the ground, but she pushed him away with her hooves as she giggled. "When did it start?" he asked.

"She had been out collecting giant Funflowers for our float in the garden earlier ..." Emerald explained. She pointed at the float, which displayed shapes of the sun and moon. "When we came back from having our lunch, she was here just like this."

"How peculiar." While Cadance couldn't determine the cause of the laughter, she knew what to do to help. "This should do the trick." She braced her hooves on the ground, summoned her magical energy and pointed her horn at Petal Shine. A swirl of blue aura floated to the pony. Within seconds, the giggles subsided.

Petal Shine stood up, confused. She looked up at the starry sky. "It's night-time? Did I fall asleep?"

"What's the last thing you remember?" Emerald Gem asked.

"I was smelling a giant Funflower to make sure it would go nicely with the other flowers on our float, and then I guess I fell asleep."

Cadance, Shining Armour and Emerald all exchanged worried looks. Funflower allergies were fairly common – even Twilight Sparkle's friend Big McIntosh had one – so perhaps the pony had simply been allergic. But a voice deep down told Cadance that there was something more to this flowery incident.

And she was going to have to get to the root of it.

CHAPTER 8

Caught Off Royal Guard

The Royal Guard hopefuls galloped back and forth, pounding their strong hooves into the dirt and grass. The field was a constellation of divots. Shining Armour stood at the helm, wearing his Royal Guard commander's uniform with pride. He barked out orders as part of a training exercise meant to prepare the stallions for anything and everything. If the ponies didn't react correctly to the order given, they were out. The exercise would continue until one stallion stood victorious.

"Right flank … MARCH!"

The stallions turned right, all except for one with a dusty-orange mane, who spun left. "Topaz, out!" called Shining Armour. The pony hung his head and trotted to the sideline to meet the others who had met a similar fate. Now there were only four ponies left in the exercise.

"About-TURN!"

Three of the stallions turned in a circle to the left instead of right as they were supposed to. Shining Armour pointed his hoof at the one pony who had performed the move correctly. He was a strong, towering golden stallion. Everypony knew he was the best, most dedicated potential soldier of the bunch.

"Jasper Hoof wins the drill-off!" The golden stallion stood to attention and didn't even crack a smile.

Princess Cadance had been secretly watching the try-outs from the stands, hoping to show a little support for Shining Armour without getting in his way. She hadn't planned on revealing herself to the stallions, but it seemed like the perfect time to give them a break.

"Darling!" Princess Cadance shouted. "How about giving the boys a breather?"

"Cady, what are you doing here?" he said through his teeth. He widened his eyes. "We've got a lot to do today …"

"Oh, come on, now, Mr Serious," Cadance teased Shining Armour.

She mimicked his tight-lipped facial expression. "You and the stallions still need to eat lunch, right? I'll have the kitchen bring down a picnic so they can check out the garden."

Over his shoulder, the princess saw the ponies' ears perk up. Even Jasper Hoof, who had been all business earlier, seemed hopeful. Shining Armour glanced back at them. "I guess they have been working really hard …" He smiled as he caved. "How do you manage to convince me of everything you want?"

The princess batted her eyelashes, innocent as ever. "I don't know … magic?"

"I'm under your spell, my dear." Shining Armour turned back to his stallions and yelled, "Let's move out, recruits! LUNCH!"

Ponies from all over the Empire were already frolicking in the revamped garden, even though the celebration was officially still a few days away. They appeared to be nothing short of entranced by the new-found natural beauty of the castle grounds. And for good reason – the flower selections were like nothing Cadance had ever seen before. The blooms were every colour of the rainbow and ranged from the size of a newborn foal to a full-grown stallion!

Some of the plants were so unique that Cadance didn't recognise them. They must only grow in the Crystal Empire.

She wanted to ask the names of the beautiful new flowers, but there was no sign of Olivine Jewel and her two friends. *Hmmm*, thought the princess. *They must finally be finished*. She made a mental note to praise them for their excellent contributions.

Cadance was filled with pride as she strolled through the garden and watched the ponies have fun. Some Crystal ponies lay in the grass, staring up at the clouds. Others laughed and some hummed upbeat tunes. A few sat mesmerised as they stared into the shimmering water of the centrepiece fountain of Spike the Brave and Glorious. The statue dragon had real emeralds for eyes and squirted water out of its mouth, a reminder of the fire the real Spike had lit in honour of the Equestria Games.

The Royal Guard hopefuls had no trouble finding a nice patch of grass to enjoy their picnic of sandwiches, made from Granny Smith's own stock of zap apple jam, shipped all the way from Sweet Apple Acres. Shining Armour laughed heartily at somepony's joke, then stopped himself and nodded, looking serious. He was doing his best to retain some sense of authority while still being one of the stallions.

A bright orange monarch butterfly landed on Cadance's muzzle for a moment and took off toward the fountain. Cadance watched its journey as it landed on the nose of a pony she recognised as Glitter Mint. But the filly didn't react to the butterfly. She just kept staring intently at something in the water.

Cadance trotted over, intrigued by the

odd behaviour. "What are you looking at, Glitter Mint?"

"Myself," the filly answered dreamily. "I'm *so* fascinating …"

"I am, too … Look at me …" mused the pony next to her. She was doing the exact same thing as Glitter Mint. "I can't stop looking at my face. It's like I've never seen it before." Her eyes bore into her watery reflection. She wasn't even blinking!

Nearby, a pair of ponies were humming so loud they sounded like a hive of bees. It wasn't a melody – just noise. The ponies had the same glazed-over look as Glitter Mint and her friend. They appeared to be having a conversation, but instead of talking, they were just humming to each other.

What? Cadance suddenly felt as if she'd entered an alternate reality. Maybe she had! She rubbed her eyes and tried to will herself out of the vision. But when the princess opened them, everything was the same as before. It was real.

Olivine, Fire Opal and Star Seed hid in one of the Humzinnia bushes nearby. The three little ponies had pegs on their muzzles to make sure they didn't accidentally sniff the flowers themselves. They watched the scene unfold in fascination and shock.

"I can't believe the enchanted flowers actually worked!" Olivine smiled in wonder. "My grandpa always told me stories of magic plants, but I thought he was making it up."

"It's actually kind of awesome!" marvelled Fire Opal. Her voice sounded nasal because of the peg. "Nice job!"

"You're *sure* nopony will be harmed?" Star Seed asked again. "It's just, like, a weird way to connect with nature?"

"Of course! They're totally fine," Olive assured them. She watched as a teal Unicorn sniffed a gigantic white Lazilily and lay down on the grass, yawning. "The effects wear off eventually." *But Princess Cadance doesn't know that,* Olivine thought. Maybe soon she would regret making a bunch of young ponies do all the work …

CHAPTER 9

Panic at the Castle

Back at the castle, word had already spread that there was some sort of funny business going on at the garden. When Cadance and Shining Armour burst through the double doors, their best staff members were already researching all the possible causes for the ponies' strange behaviour.

The advisors were gathered around a table covered with a hundred books pulled from the Crystal Empire Library.

"Any ideas?" Princess Cadance looked to the group, feeling panicked. "I've never seen anything this … *bizarre*."

"It's definitely Discord!" Shimmer Berry shouted, pointing to a picture of the draconequus in an old tome entitled *The Chaotic Age of Equestria*. "This has all his trademarks! Silly sights, silly sounds, silly smells …"

"The changelings are here!" cried Lieutenant Jade Wing as he flipped through a book on Queen Chrysalis. "And they're impersonating our friends. Don't changelings hum? I think I read that in here somewhere …"

"King Sombra is back," whispered the butler pony, looking frightened.

"He's going to suck all the love out of the Empire again ..."

"Whatever it is, we need a solution." Shining Armour furrowed his brow in frustration. "Fast." He was particularly annoyed because his entire team of recruits was now acting strange, too. The nimble stallions had suddenly become clumsy and uncoordinated. Jasper Hoof had tripped over his horseshoes when Shining Armour had called the ponies to stand at attention.

"I don't think it's a plot by an evil force," Cadance thought aloud. "It's more harmless than that ..." She paced back and forth. "It seems like the work of an individual."

"That doesn't make sense. What sort of grumpy pony would want to sabotage the Garden Hearts Celebration?" wondered Shimmer Berry out loud.

Suddenly, an image of Olivine Jewel frowning at the back of the school group flashed in Cadance's mind. "Perhaps it was somepony who wanted to stand out ..."

"What do you mean?" A puzzled Shining Armour cocked his head to the side. "Do you know who did this, Cady?"

"I think I do," Princess Cadance said, nodding. "It's all my fault. I'm going to find her and set everything straight."

Before anypony could protest, the princess was galloping out the door in a flash of pink and gold.

Chapter 10

The Crystal Crown Café

"Olivine Jewel!" Princess Cadance called out over the cacophony of hums, giggles and snores of the enchanted ponies in the garden. "Are you there, Olivine? I need to talk to you!" She trotted through the hedge maze and past the row of beautiful topiaries cut into the shapes of animals.

The sight reminded her of the vision – the whole reason why Cadance had pushed this plan into action.

"It's worse." Cadance hung her head as she approached a pair of ponies giggling uncontrollably, just as Petal Shine had. Cadance summoned her magic and directed it at them. But, unfortunately, the spell the ponies were under was too strong, and their wild fits of laughter continued.

"Oh, Celestia, what have I done?" Princess Cadance sighed. She kept walking, half-heartedly looking for the little green filly.

The problem with glimpses of the future, she thought, was that they were incomplete pictures. How was the princess to know that behind the sound of pony laughter she'd heard was some sort of spell forcing them to giggle at everything? Cadance now realised she had been twisting the vision to suit her own desires. It was about as helpful as trying to decipher a pattern of leaves in the bottom of her teacup.

Cadance took a sip of the piping hot dandelion tea. "Thank you for the tea, Lilac Quartz, but I really can't stay." The princess had come to the café only to look for Olivine, but she'd been ushered to the best table.

"Your Majesty, I insist!" the motherly mare fussed. She carried over a platter of warm Crystal berry tarts and placed them gingerly on the table. "At least have a tart before you go."

Cadance shoved a tart into her mouth and spoke through the crumbly sweetness. "Have you seen your daughter? It's urgent that I find her …"

"I have just one more treat for you, Princess!" Lilac Quartz trotted to the kitchen in the back, ignoring the question.

"What's that Olivine done now?" a mare whispered, leaning in from the next table. Cadance recognised her from the day of the Heartsong. Her name was Sweet Leaf. "Poor Lilac Quartz can't even rein her filly in …" Sweet Leaf said.

Across from her, another mare from their group that day – Rose Water – shook her head. "That little pony is up to something bad."

"Whatever do you mean?" Cadance asked.

The princess was growing impatient. The sooner she found Olivine, the sooner she would solve the mystery in the garden. The princess knew she was on the right track. Olivine had been down in the area the entire time. She must have seen – or done – something.

"My sweet little Star Seed wouldn't do anything wrong." Sweet Leaf nodded. "She's always been a model student."

These two gossips weren't Princess Cadance's cup of tea at all.

"Excuse me, ladies." Princess Cadance stood up. "I'm actually here to speak to Lilac Quartz about a special honour that Olivine Jewel is going to be given by the castle." The two mares' jaws dropped. "Good day."

CHAPTER 11

Master Gardener Alabaster Stone

Even though the princess had sent word to the castle that she might be gone for a few hours, Cadance didn't think her investigation would lead her all the way to the outskirts of the Crystal Empire.

But here she was, behind Lilac Quartz, stomping through the wild foliage to an old cottage.

"Olivine Jewel comes here all the time to visit her grandfather Alabaster Stone," Lilac Quartz explained. "She's quite attached to him. Loves his old stories about the Crystal Empire before King Sombra." Lilac made a sad face. "When he can remember them, that is …"

"It's so isolated out here," Cadance observed. "Why doesn't he live closer to the centre of the Crystal Empire?"

Lilac Quartz motioned to all the overgrown plants in crystal pots on the porch. "He's got more room for his plants out here." She smiled. "He doesn't grow half as much as he used to, but he's still got the same spirit that he had all those years ago when he worked at the castle."

The mare twisted the knob and shoved open the heavy wooden door. "But I'm sure Olivine told you all about that."

"No, she didn't mention it …" Princess Cadance narrowed her eyes. "Alabaster worked in the castle garden?"

"Oh, yes! He was the greatest pony in all of Equestria at what he did," Lilac Quartz replied. "They even did an interview with him in the Equestrian Botanical Society journal – 'Flora and Foalna' – about the southern plants he was able to grow in the Crystal climate!"

As Cadance followed Lilac inside, she saw evidence of the stallion's long and illustrious career. The warm cottage was packed full with plants and memorabilia.

Her eyes landed on a framed photo. The image was yellowed from age but clear – it was a young Alabaster standing proudly next to a familiar sign that read, EMPIRE GARDEN, BY MASTER GARDENER "A.S."

"So *he's* the famous master gardener! Wow." Cadance brightened. "'A.S.' stands for 'Alabaster Stone'."

"Who's askin'?" grumbled the old stallion, waking up from a nap in his cosy chair. "I didn't do it." He coughed. "What?"

"Hi, Dad!" Lilac trotted over, setting down the basket of Crystal Crown Café goodies she'd brought over for him. "This is Her Majesty, Princess Cadance!"

Cadance gave a friendly bow.

Alabaster frowned. "Princess, huh?"

"Olive didn't tell you she was helping to fix the castle gardens for the big Garden Hearts Celebration?"

"No," answered Alabaster Stone. "But she shouldn't be. Those royals—"

"Be nice, please?" Lilac interrupted through gritted teeth. "We're looking for Olivine. Have you seen her today?"

"It could have been today … coulda been a week ago." He scratched his thin white mane with his hoof. The stallion stood up slowly and began to shuffle toward the kitchen. "She was here with a couple of little fillies. But I was havin' my nap, so I didn't get up." Alabaster pointed to his bookshelf. "They were nosin' through my stuff, though."

"Did Olivine or the other ponies happen to take anything?" asked Princess

Cadance, scanning the cluttered room. It would probably be hard to notice anything missing. Perhaps they'd borrowed some of Alabaster's gardening tools. There were certainly plenty to choose from here.

"How should I know?" Alabaster grunted. "Look at this place!" He began to fix himself a bowl of oats. "At least the only thing I have of value is safe. Right there on the brown table in the corner."

Lilac Quartz trotted over to the table in question. There was nothing on it but dust and a clean square space. "Are you sure, Dad? Your enchanted seed box … well, it's gone."

"What!" Alabaster shuffled his hooves as fast as he could. "But … it's dangerous." The colour drained from his face. "Daffospills … and Reflection Roses …?

Giggling Funflowers, Humzinnias, *and* Lazililies? If anypony plants those seeds and smells those flowers, we're going to have a major problem on our hooves."

Princess Cadance thought of the ponies trapped in the garden. "I think we already do." She gulped. "Mr Stone, can you help us fix it?"

"I, I … would, but I …" the old pony stammered, putting his hoof to his head. "I can't remember how."

CHAPTER 12

Crystal Blue Persuasion

On their frantic trip back to the castle, the trio passed by the Crystal Heart. Much to the princess's dismay, the light was now at a constant flicker. In her own heart, Cadance knew that it was getting worse because of all the citizens who were under the spell of the magical flowers.

How could a pony embody true light and love when they were in an altered state of mind? It was impossible. Cadance couldn't believe the mess that she'd made of everything.

"Hurry! It's not far!" Princess Cadance called over her shoulder. "Mr Stone, I just know that if you step hoof in the garden, it'll help you remember something." She forged ahead across the grassy field with Alabaster and Lilac Quartz in tow. The old stallion hadn't stopped complaining the whole time.

"The castle doesn't deserve my help," Alabaster muttered to his daughter. "They didn't want me back after King Sombra was defeated!"

"Nonsense, Dad." Lilac Quartz frowned. "*You* told them it would be too much work to fix the garden again."

"Hogwash!" Alabaster replied, raising a bushy eyebrow. "That's not how I remember it …"

"My point exactly," Lilac Quartz teased, then tried an alternative approach. She batted her big, aqua-coloured eyes at him. "Just try to help out for Olivine, OK?"

A loud noise began to drown out their conversation as the three ponies arrived at the garden gates. In Princess Cadance's absence, the problem had multiplied tenfold. There were now hundreds of ponies trotting around the area in various states of enchantment.

Unicorns, Pegasi and Earth ponies of all ages hummed and giggled, lounged and stared at themselves in the fountain. The swaths of ribbons and lights, along with the brilliant colours of the flowers, gave the whole scene a sense of festivity.

But this was no party – this was a disaster! Cadance wished that Sunburst, the Crystal Empire's most knowledgeable pony on the topic of ancient spells, wasn't visiting  his friend Starlight Glimmer in Ponyville right now. Sunburst might know what to do … because Alabaster Stone clearly didn't.

"Jumpin' juniper berries!" Alabaster marvelled, his hooves frozen in place. His eyes were wide with awe. "My garden is amazin'. Look at the ponies! Look at the flowers! My magic seeds are just as pretty as I always imagined they'd be …"

"Dad! Focus!" Lilac Quartz motioned to the ponies with her purple hoof. "What do we do to break the spells?"

"I've got it! We sing!" Alabaster whipped his head around. "That'll do the trick!" He trotted past a group of ponies lounging on the grass and toward a vibrant orange Humzinnia plant. *"Tra-la-la-la, hello, little Humzinniaaa!"* the old stallion sang with glee. He leaned down to sniff the flower.

"*Noooo*, Grandpa!" Olivine Jewel shouted, galloping toward him. "Don't smell it!" The young green mare tried to push Alabaster out of the way, but it was too late. The stallion stood up with a smile on his face and a hum on his lips.

"I'm so sorry, Princess Cadance," Olivine whimpered as she sank to the ground, defeated. She was still wearing the clothes-pin on her muzzle, which explained how she had not been affected. "This is all my fault."

"That doesn't matter right now."
Princess Cadance shook her head. "Right
now we have to fix this. I'm going to fetch
Shining Armour. Maybe he and his Royal
Guard are on their way!"

"Oh, uh … Princess?" Lilac Quartz bit
her lip and pointed straight ahead.
"I think that ship has sailed, dear." Sure
enough, Shining Armour was there,
surrounded by his guards. But there was
no rescue mission under way. Instead, the
uniformed, burly stallions were giggling
like a Filly Scout troop at a slumber party.

"Shining Armour!" Cadance cried out
in anguish. "Don't worry,
boys! I'll save you!"
Cadance calmly began
to rack her brains for
spells that might help,
but she couldn't think.

If only she could recall her vision and look closer. She had to be missing something …

"I have an idea," Cadance announced, springing to action. "I'll be right back." She took off into the air.

Just outside the garden, in the exact spot her vision had depicted, the princess made one last attempt. Cadance closed her eyes, painting the picture in her mind. Everything melted away, and there she was again in the dream state: the lush green grass and the sun shining on her pink face, the fresh air, and the heavy scent of flower blossoms. In the distance, intricate topiaries lined the horizon. Hundreds of ponies were singing.

Hundreds of ponies were singing!

"That's it!" Cadance shouted as she snapped out of her vision. She could almost hear Princess Luna's voice in her head as she recited an old sorcery saying: *When the spell is strong and has been far prolonged, a familiar song may right the wrong.*

The heartsong! It was worth a try.

The pink Alicorn took off, spreading her purple-tipped wings and soaring back to the heart of the commotion. She floated above the garden and focused her energy. A soft blue haze of magical aura from her horn surrounded her neck to amplify her voice.

Then the princess began to sing with all her heart.

"When the Crystal snow is no longer chilly, join voices with every colt and every filly!"

As she sang, two or three ponies craned their necks and looked up at her.

Cadance's pulse quickened with excitement. It was working! She kept singing. *"There's only one solution, and we've made a resolution …"* Her pretty voice rang out, awakening even more confused ponies. Some of them began to join in. The sound grew stronger and richer with each note.

"We'll lift our spirits to the sky. Our hearts grow full and our hooves rise up high." The rest of the spellbound citizens snapped back to reality. More and more ponies joined in the song. *"Hooves cold, hearts warm; cold hooves, warm hearts! Garden Hearts, we all take paaaaaart!"*

A searing flash of blue light washed over everything as Cadance felt her body plummeting to the ground. The spell was broken and the Crystal Heart had been powered once more!

CHAPTER 13

The Horse Awakens

The sound of birds was the first thing
Cadance noticed. No humming, no
incessant laughter – just the sweet song
and twittering of the birds. And whispers.
She blinked and rubbed away the
remnants of the bright light. Cadance
opened her eyes to a crowd of curious

ponies standing around, scratching their heads and trying to piece together what exactly had happened.

"Why are we in the garden?" wondered Jasper Hoof, looking around.

"Did I fall asleep?" asked Glitter Mint, rubbing her eyes.

"Is the princess OK?" Gemma called out, standing on her tippy-hooves to see.

"Cady!" Shining Armour rushed over to his wife, breaking through the mob of Crystal ponies. He helped her up from the ground. "You did it! You saved everypony! I don't know how … but one minute I was leading my stallions to practice, and the next I was singing 'Cold Hooves, Warm Hearts' with you flying above us." He gestured to the crowd. "I have a feeling there was a lot more between that …"

"You have no idea." Cadance smiled.

What a relief! Her citizens were freed from the spell, and nopony was hurt. Her eyes scanned the crowd and landed on a particular young green filly who was hunched over in the dirt. Her pink mane was hanging down over her eyes, and she was sniffling.

"Olive!" Lilac Quartz reprimanded, approaching her daughter. "Why in Equestria would you steal Grandpa's seeds?" The mother's face was flushed with embarrassment. "You nearly caused the entire Crystal Empire to be trapped in their enchantments for ever!"

"I know," Olive said, and sniffed. "I'm so sorry, Mama. I didn't think it would end up like this …" Olive stood up and shrugged. "All I wanted was a little bit of revenge."

"Revenge?" Princess Cadance asked as she walked towards them. "I don't understand … Who has wronged you, Olivine Jewel?"

"At first I was annoyed at *you*, Princess Cadance …" Olivine admitted.

Everypony gasped.

Cadance slumped down. "But why?"

Olive's face twisted into a frown. "All this time after the Crystal Empire returned and you've never even offered Grandpa his job back!" Olivine paced, motioning with her hooves. "And then you force *me* of all ponies to fix his garden?"

"I didn't even know—"

"But everypony else loved doing the castle's dirty work. They were having so much fun digging and planting seeds! And, as usual, I was alone in a corner."

Olivine pointed to Star Seed and Fire Opal. "I just wanted to be more like them. I wanted them to like *me* … I realised I had the perfect way to impress everypony."

"My magic seed collection?" Grandpa Alabaster coughed. "You know better than that, Little 'Vine." Olive looked down at her hooves in shame.

"You didn't need to do that to impress us," Star Seed laughed. "All you had to do was, like, chill out."

"Seriously," Fire Opal agreed, flipping her rainbow mane. "We liked you before, and we won't stop now."

Olivine's eyes grew huge. "Really?"

"Of course!" Star Seed and Fire Opal embraced their new friend in a hug.

Olivine turned to Princess Cadance. "I can't believe I made so many huge mistakes. I'm so sorry, Princess."

The filly took a deep breath. "I
understand if you want to ban me from
the Crystal Empire—"

"What?" Princess
Cadance interrupted.
She couldn't help but
chuckle. "Oh, Olivine
Jewel ... *I'm* the one
who should be
apologising to you. I saw that
something was bothering you at the
Hearts and Hooves Day Heartsong, and I
didn't even bother to dig deeper. I should
have asked what the root of the problem
was, instead of assuming I could solve it."
Princess Cadance put her hoof on Olive's
shoulder. "I feel that this mess has been
both of our doing. So what do you say
to getting the garden ready for the
big celebration tomorrow ... together?"

Cadance extended her pink hoof.

"I would love that." Olivine laughed with relief. She hoof-bumped Cadance. "The funny thing is … through all of this, I found out that I actually really enjoy gardening. A lot."

Lilac Quartz rolled her eyes. "I've been telling you that for years!"

"Me too!" Grandpa Alabaster grunted with a satisfied smirk. "Always had the talent."

"What can I say?" Olivine smiled and shrugged. "Sometimes a filly has got to sow her own oats to figure it out, even if the seeds were planted early on."

Olivine trotted over to a bush covered in brilliant red roses. She plucked one and presented it to Princess Cadance. "I grew this one by myself. No magic spells." She smiled wide with pride.

Cadance held the bloom to her muzzle and inhaled. The sweet scent was fresh and pure. "It's perfect."

"And so is your cutie mark!" Fire Opal pointed at the pony's flank. Sure enough, resting on Olivine Jewel's flank was a beautiful cutie mark of a green heart-shaped jewel. It looked almost like the Crystal Heart itself, but it had swirly, curly green vines growing around it. "It looks almost like ... *a Garden Heart.*"

CHAPTER 14

Garden Heart Celebrations

Flower petals fell from the sky in a rainbow of colours. They fluttered on to the ponies, sticking to their manes and covering the shimmering crystal ground in a soft, fragrant carpet. Olivine Jewel could hardly believe that she was sitting on the royal float with baby Flurry Heart, right between Princess Cadance and Prince Shining Armour, as Grand Mareshall of the Garden Hearts Celebration Parade. The Crystal Heart shone brightly on a platform below them, surrounded by hundreds of blue and white flowers. It felt like a dream.

"Princess Cadance?" Olivine asked, throwing a hoof-ful of fresh petals on to the crowd below. She could see her mother, Lilac Quartz, standing next to a very grumpy Sweet Leaf and Rose Water.

"Happy Spring!" Princess Cadance waved her hoof. "Yes, Olivine?"

"Why did you choose me to be Grand Mareshall? After everything I did?"

Princess Cadance laughed. "You're the pony who reminds me of spring."

"I am?" Olivine scrunched up her muzzle in surprise. "Why?"

"Because no matter how cold the winter – or how big our mistakes – may be, there is always time to start afresh again." Cadance grinned and gave Olivine a nudge. "Don't you agree?" For the first time ever, Olivine did. Her Crystal heart had finally bloomed, right along with the flowers. And after watching Olivine grow, Cadance was brimming with light and love.

Read on for a sneak peek
at the next exciting
My Little Pony adventure,

Lyra and the Secret Agent Ponies

"Thanks for going with me to the party, Bon Bon," said Lyra as she followed her best friend into the cottage. Lyra, a mint-green Unicorn, broke into a tiny smile.

"It was nothing, really," replied Bon Bon, distractedly. She trotted around the room, looking under furniture and opening cupboards.

"Stop." Lyra put her hoof on Bon Bon's shoulder and caught her eye. "It meant a lot to me. I know how you hate big social events like that, even when they are thrown by Ponyville's best party planner – Pinkie Pie."

Lyra reflected on the party, riffling through the snapshots in her mind of fun Hearts and Hooves Day activities. There had been cards, songs, heart-shaped confetti, and chocolate treats as far as the eye could see. They had played a game where everypony tried to guess the new filling flavours of the truffles that Pinkie Pie had whipped up especially for the party. Bon Bon had won by guessing "caramarshmallow sprinkle," but seemed quite embarrassed about it – she had demanded they make a quick exit right after.

"The party was fine, but I just don't enjoy small talk like you do, Lyra." Bon Bon sighed deeply as she latched the double lock on the door. Her eyes darted to the front window. The curtains were open, letting the light in.

Bon Bon suppressed the urge to canter over and close them immediately. Lyra preferred a bright cottage when she visited. "I'm a product of my past, it seems. No personal details allowed."

Lyra giggled. "You mean your *secret* past as one of Equestria's top monster-fighting secret agents?" She had recently found out the truth about her best friend.

"Shhhh!" Bon Bon hissed as she looked around the small, unoccupied room. "They could have it bugged," Bon Bon snapped. "Somepony is *always* listening."

"Sorry, I forgot." Lyra rolled her eyes. "But you're being a little bit paranoid. Besides, all that secret monster stuff is behind you now!"

"Where?" Bon Bon whipped around.

Lyra rolled her eyes again. "Can we just move on to our own Hearts and Hooves Day tradition now?"

"Hearts and Hooves frozen hot chocolate? Sure. Yeah, good idea." The two ponies trotted to the kitchen. *Maybe Lyra is right,* thought Bon Bon. She really needed to calm down. Nopony (or monster) was out to get her. She was safe here in Ponyville, living her simple life and watching her best buddy whip up a yummy treat.

Bon Bon plopped down at the dining table and took a deep breath. *Act normal,* she told herself. *You did before Lyra found out the truth.* "I'm surprised you want to have any more chocolate today!"

"There's no such thing as too much chocolate." Lyra opened the icebox and began to prepare the drinks.

"I'm so glad you taught me how to make this. Where did you find the recipe?" asked Lyra. She used her magic to pour chocolate into a mixing bowl. "I always forget!"

"At the agency, actually." Bon Bon grinned, recalling the day. "The gang and I were doing some experiments with cryogenic freezing when somepony accidentally zapped a cup of hot chocolate! It made the most delicious drink ever." Bon Bon laughed. "We tried to replicate it, but only the Unicorns on the team could do it. So we came up with this version, which doesn't require a freeze zap. Just ice and a good shaker."

"You told me you learned it at college!" Lyra teased. She shook the ice and chocolate around in the shaker. It rattled noisily.
"I swear, Bon Bon. It's like getting to know you all over again …"

Bon Bon looked down at her hooves.
Poor Lyra.

"Which is kind of awesome," Lyra added with a wink.

Bon Bon breathed a huge sigh of relief.

"I'm so lucky to have somepony in my life who is as understanding as you are, Lyra. Even after all the lies."

"Well, I hope things never change!" Lyra replied, passing a frosty mug of frozen hot chocolate to her buddy. The two ponies held up their mugs.

"To being best friends forever!" they cheered in unison.

They had barely clinked their drinks when a loud knock rattled the door. *Thump, thump, thump!* The commotion nearly knocked it clean off its hinges. *Thump, thump, thump!*

Read

Lyra and the
Secret Agent Ponies

to find out what happens next!

Turn the page for a special surprise from Princess Cadance ...

Dear Reader,

I created these bonus pages just for you while Flurry Heart was down for her nap! Enjoy the activities and share them with your friends.

Love,

Princess Cadance

An A-Maze-ing Garden

The ponies of Crystal Prep have been working so hard to help Princess Cadance fix up the Crystal Empire Gardens. Along with planting beautiful flowers, they have decided to design a hedge maze! Can you help Princess Cadance find her way through the hedges back to the castle?

Start

Finish

Colours of Your Crystal Heart

Princess Cadance has a problem! The glittering Crystal Heart is looking a little bit dull today. It should be filled with rainbow colours and sparkling light. Can you help the love shine through by colouring in the heart?

On Guard!

Shining Armour takes great pride in training his
Royal Guard stallions to be the very best in Equestria.
They play all sorts of games and do exercises to make
sure that they are strong and ready for *anything*.
Shining Armour loves each soldier's individuality, but
when they are a team they must look uniform.
Can you help Shining Armour get his guards in
line by circling the differences below?

example

SPREAD THE LOVE

The Crystal Empire is powered by the magical
Crystal Heart, which runs on the love and positive
feelings of the ponies. In addition to events
like the Heartsong, everypony likes to compliment
one another. It makes them feel wonderful!
Use the space below to write some compliments
about the friends and family members in
your life. Then let them know how you feel,
to spread light and love like a Crystal Pony!

Name: _____

Compliment: _____

_____

Name: _____

Compliment: _____

_____

Name: _____

Compliment: _____

_____

A Garden of Friends

Strong friendships can take time to grow. Sometimes you have to plant the seeds of friendship and help them along with silly jokes and fun times together! Think about a friend and write about them here. What makes this friend so special to you? How have you grown with them?

_____

_____

_____

_____

_____

_____

_____

_____

_____

_____

_____

_____

Heartsongs and Sing-alongs

The Hearts and Hooves Day Heartsong is only one of the many traditions the Crystal Ponies uphold in their land. At this event, the ponies join together in song to show their love for one another and for their beautiful home. What is your favourite song to sing? Choose one that makes you feel happy, and write the lyrics here!

Name of song: _____

Artist: _____

I like this song because: _____

_____

_____

_____

Lyrics: _____

_____

_____

_____

_____

_____

A Grand Time Together

In the story, the young pony Olivine Jewel has a special relationship with her grandpa, Alabaster Stone. She loves listening to everything he knows about plants and gardening, as well as just talking to him over a cup of hot cocoa. Do you have a grandparent or an adult in your life that you like to spend time with? If so, what is your favourite activity to do with them? What's the most interesting fact they've told you? Write about them below.

_____

_____

_____

_____

_____

_____

_____

_____

_____

_____

Digging for Words

The Crystal Ponies were so busy digging in the garden that they didn't realise they covered up these words with dirt! Can you help the ponies unearth the words below? Circle each one. *Hint:* they can be found running forwards, backwards, up, down, and diagonally!

CADANCE

CRYSTAL

FLOWER

GARDEN

PRINCESS

LOVE

OLIVINE

HEARTSONG

```
H P K E K E F E T K A N
A R E W O L F Y L P O D
A I V R M M C G S R J I
G N O S T R A E H N E C
I C L Y N O C S S E Y E
Q E R S A N E L W I E I
L S R Y A G A R D E N M
L S C D S K U D H O T M
R A A I G T H E G N N C
E C K F S C A N R E G S
P P E N I V I L O D C E
```

Floating on Flowers

Princess Cadance has a wonderful idea to include a parade in her spring celebration. All the ponies are invited to create floats covered entirely in fresh flowers. If you were designing a float for Cadance's parade, what would it look like? Draw it below. Don't forget to include lots of colourful flowers!

A Rose by Any Other Name

Shining Armour loves to tease his wife by calling her "Mi Amore Cadenza," which is really her full name! But the princess prefers her nickname, "Cadance". Can you connect the names of the ponies below with their nicknames?

Twilight Sparkle

Celestia

Applejack

Olivine Jewel

Rainbow Dash

"A.J."

"Twiley"

"Olive"

"Dashie"

"Celie"

Grow Your Garden

Spring is a glorious season! After the long, cold winter, the sun comes out and plants begin to grow again. Have you ever tried to grow anything? Ask an adult to help you plant some seeds and use the space below to record their progress. You can plant flowers, vegetables, or even herbs for cooking!

Name of Plant:

Draw a Picture of the Seed Here:

Date Planted: _____

This Plant Should Be
Watered Every: _____

Week 1: _____
_____
_____

Week 2: _____
_____
_____

Week 3: _____
_____
_____

DRAW a PICTURE of YOUR PLANT HERE: